Read all the titles in this series

MARY POPE OSBORNE'S
TALES FROM THE
ODYSSEY

Circe's
Island

The
Sirens

Island of
Aeolus

Scylla

Cyclops'
Cave

Island of
the Sun God

Charybdis

Land of the Dead

Calypso's
Island

Land of the
Lotus Eaters

Oceanus

GREECE

Troy

CRETE

T·H·02

MARY POPE OSBORNE'S

TALES FROM THE

ODYSSEY

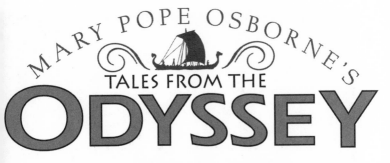

MARY POPE OSBORNE'S
TALES FROM THE
ODYSSEY

Book Six

THE FINAL BATTLE

By **MARY POPE OSBORNE**
With artwork by **TROY HOWELL**

Hyperion Paperbacks for Children   New York

To Donna Bray with gratitude
for taking the journey with me

Special thanks to Frederick J. Booth, Ph.D.,
Professor of Classical Studies, Seton Hall University,
for his expert advice

Text copyright © 2004 by Mary Pope Osborne
Artwork copyright © 2004 by Troy Howell

First Hyperion Paperback edition, 2005
1 3 5 7 9 10 8 6 4 2
Printed in the United States of America
Library of Congress Cataloging-in-Publication Data on file.
ISBN 0-7868-0994-9 (pbk.)
Visit www.hyperionbooksforchildren.com

CONTENTS

PROLOGUE

In the early morning of time, there existed a mysterious world called Mount Olympus. Hidden behind a veil of clouds, this world was never swept by winds, nor washed by rains. Those who lived on Mount Olympus never grew old; they never died. They were not humans. They were the mighty gods and goddesses of ancient Greece.

The Olympian gods and goddesses had great power over the lives of the humans who lived on earth below. Their anger once caused a man named Odysseus to wander the seas for many long years, trying to find his way home.

Almost three thousand years ago, a Greek poet named Homer first told the story of Odysseus' journey. Since that time, storytellers have told the strange and wondrous tale again and again. We call that story the Odyssey.

PENELOPE

*P*enelope, queen of Ithaca, wept and prayed to the gods as she waited for news of her son, Telemachus. Five weeks earlier, the young man had sailed away in search of his long-lost father, Odysseus. Shortly after his departure, Penelope had learned that her suitors were plotting to murder her son on his journey home.

For years, these wicked men had tried to take Odysseus' place. They tormented Penelope daily, invading her home and demanding that she choose one of them for a husband. But Penelope remained fiercely loyal to Odysseus. Enduring threats and humiliation, she had led the suitors on with false promises of marriage, then put them off again and again by refusing to choose whom to wed.

Now Penelope wept for both

Odysseus and Telemachus. As she paced in her chamber, she heard some-one calling to her from the courtyard below. Penelope rushed to the window and saw the old swineherd who lived on the pig farm near the shore. The swineherd was surrounded by Penelope's servants and suitors.

"My lady, weep no more," the swine-herd called to Penelope. "Your son is safe! Yesterday his ship docked at our island. He rests now at my hut."

Hearing this news, Penelope and her handmaidens wept tears of joy. But the suitors were plainly unhappy to hear that Telemachus had returned safely to Ithaca. When Penelope learned they were making a new plot to kill her son, she went downstairs to confront them. Filled with fury, she called out to Antinous, the leader of the villains.

"Antinous! Do you not remember how my husband once saved your father from an angry mob?" Penelope said. "And now you try to take Odysseus' place and murder his son! How dare you?"

Before Antinous could answer, one of

the other suitors called out from the crowd, "Do not worry, Queen Penelope! Your son has nothing to fear from us. Of course, should the gods decree that he die, there is nothing we can do."

Helpless in the face of their evil, Penelope could say no more. She returned to her chamber. She wept bitter tears for her husband and son, until finally the gray-eyed goddess, Athena, closed Penelope's eyelids and gave her the gift of sleep.

APPROACH TO THE PALACE

$\mathcal{J}$he goddess Athena was also watching over Odysseus and Telemachus. Just two days before, Athena had helped Odysseus return to the shores of Ithaca and disguised him as a beggar.

When Odysseus had hobbled to the hut of his faithful swineherd, the old man had not recognized him. Later, when Telemachus arrived at the hut, he also did not recognize Odysseus. But when father and son were alone, Athena magically took away Odysseus' disguise. Since their joyful reunion, Odysseus and Telemachus had been making a plan to fight the suitors, whose number exceeded one hundred.

Now, huddled near an evening campfire, father and son reviewed their plot. "You will go to the palace first,"

Odysseus said. "I will follow, in my disguise as a beggar. Remember, you must not show any sign that you know me—even if someone tries to do me harm."

"And you will tell me when it is time to hide the weapons?" asked Telemachus.

"Yes," said Odysseus. "Athena has promised to help us. When she appears and gives me the sign, we will take the spears and shields from the hall and hide them in a storeroom upstairs."

Their discussion was interrupted by the return of the swineherd. Athena's magic again gave Odysseus the appearance of a lowly beggar. As the three men prepared their supper together, father and son held their plan close to their hearts.

❖   ❖   ❖

The next morning, at the first light of dawn, Telemachus left the swineherd's hut. His mind was filled with thoughts of the coming fight as he hurried down the rocky path toward his home.

When Telemachus reached the palace, his old nurse, Euryclea, greeted him joyfully. The other maids of the house surrounded him and embraced him.

Soon his mother appeared. She threw her arms around him and wept.

"Sweet light of my eyes!" Penelope cried. "I feared I would never see you again!"

"I have traveled far, Mother—as far as the kingdom of Sparta," said Telemachus. "King Menelaus and Queen Helen showed me great hospitality there and showered me with gifts."

"And what news do you bring of your father?" Penelope asked.

Telemachus looked at his mother sadly, remembering his promise to Odysseus to tell no one of his father's return to

Ithaca. "I know only this," he said softly. "King Menelaus said that long ago the Old Man of the Sea revealed to him that Odysseus was being held captive on the island of the goddess Calypso. He cannot leave, because he no longer has any ships to carry him home."

As Telemachus told his mother more about his journey, Odysseus was heading toward the palace. Accompanied by the swineherd, he hobbled down the rocky road in his disguise.

As they neared the palace gates, Odysseus saw an old, bony dog lying on a garbage heap. Tears came to Odysseus' eyes, for he recognized the dog as his beloved hound, Argus.

When Argus caught sight of Odysseus, he seemed to recognize his master. The old dog was so feeble he could not stand. But he joyfully wagged his tail.

It pained Odysseus that he could not go to Argus, lest he give himself away. "Why does that hound lie abandoned and uncared for?" he asked the swine-herd. "He looks as if he were once a fine animal."

"Aye, he was once the master's favorite," the swineherd said. "But with the palace in such disorder, no one thinks to care for him anymore. For years, he has waited faithfully to lay eyes upon his beloved master again. He knows not that Odysseus died long ago."

As Odysseus sadly followed the swineherd through the palace gates, the old dog closed his eyes and quietly passed into the peace and darkness of death. His greatest wish had finally come true: his master had come home.

THREE

THE BEGGAR AT THE TABLE

$\mathcal{L}$eaning on his stick and covered by his ragged cloak, Odysseus stood at the threshold of the palace that had been his home twenty years before.

Soon the suitors began boisterously

invading the great hall. Invisible to the rude men, the goddess Athena appeared to Odysseus and whispered in his ear. "Go around the room and beg from each man," she said, "and you will learn who is good and who is evil."

Odysseus followed her bidding and began hobbling from man to man, begging for food.

Antinous, the leader of the suitors, took an immediate dislike to him. "What a loathsome creature you are!" he said when Odysseus approached him. "How dare you try to take our dinner?"

Odysseus looked Antinous in the eye. "And what about you, sir?" he said. "Do you not feed yourself from another man's table?"

Antinous picked up a stool and hurled it at Odysseus, striking him on the back. Odysseus took the blow silently and walked away.

Telemachus struggled against his fierce desire to defend his father, for he knew he must not reveal the beggar's true identity. But when servants told Penelope about the attack on the poor ragged man, she was furious.

"I hope the god Apollo strikes Antinous dead!" she said. "All my suitors are loathsome, but Antinous is the worst! Bring the stranger to me. Perhaps he has heard something about my husband. He seems like a man who has traveled far and seen much."

The servant hurried to relay the message to Odysseus.

"Tell your queen that I will come to her after dark," said Odysseus, "and bring her news of her husband."

While Odysseus waited for the day's end, the suitors filled the courtyard of the palace with loud singing and dancing. They quarreled and fought with one another. They shouted insults at Odysseus and threatened him.

Finally Telemachus could bear them no more. "Are you mad?" he shouted. "Have evil spirits possessed you? Leave this palace at once!"

The suitors were amazed by the young man's boldness. But, grumbling, they finally did as Telemachus commanded and took their leave.

When all the suitors had left the palace, the goddess Athena made a sign to

Odysseus. Odysseus went immediately to Telemachus. "We must prepare now for tomorrow's battle," he said. "We will remove the armor and spears from the downstairs hall. If anyone asks you why we are doing this, say that you fear they are being damaged by the heat and smoke of the household fires."

Holding a golden lamp, Athena, now invisible, led Odysseus and Telemachus through the downstairs hall. The lamp's soft glow shone upon the walls and rafters. With the help of Athena's light, father and son removed helmets, shields, and spears from the walls and carried them to an upstairs storeroom.

Then Odysseus bid good night to Telemachus. "Go to bed, my son," he said gently. "Rest for tomorrow's battle. I must go now and speak with your mother."

THE NIGHT BEFORE
THE BATTLE

Dark had descended and the palace was quiet. Queen Penelope sat in her ivory-and-silver chair by the fire of the great hall. Her beauty shone like that of the golden goddess, Aphrodite.

"Please bring a bench so my guest will be comfortable," she said to her maids.

A bench was brought and covered with a soft sheepskin. Then a servant bid Odysseus to come before the queen.

"Welcome, my friend," Penelope said. "Now, please tell me—who are you? Where do you come from? Where is your family?"

His face hidden by his ragged cloak, Odysseus spoke in a low voice: "Honorable wife of Odysseus, please do not ask me of my homeland or my family.

Do not force me to remember my pain and grief."

"I understand," said Penelope. "My own grief began twenty years ago when my husband left to fight the Trojan War. For many years now, men have come to court me. They have taken over our house. They tell me Odysseus is surely dead and demand that I choose one of them to marry.

"I tried to trick them for a while. I told them I would marry again when I had finished weaving a shroud for Odysseus' father. I worked on the shroud every day. But every night I unraveled my day's weaving, so the work would never be done.

"After three years of this trickery, a serving maid discovered my secret and told the suitors of my deceit. I had no choice but to finish my weaving. Now, they demand that I keep my word and choose one of them for a husband. I know not what to do. My years of grief and worry have left me with no more strength to fight these men."

Penelope sighed deeply. "There," she said. "I have told you of my family and my grief and my torment. Now, speak to me about yourself. Where are you from? I know you were not born from a rock or a tree."

Odysseus did not blink as he began to spin a tale for his wife. "I lived on the island of Crete," he said. "My grandfather was the great King Minos. I remember a time when your husband Odysseus was blown off course on his way to Troy, and he came to our island. I entertained him at the palace. He and his men stayed with us for twelve days. Then they put out to sea again."

Hearing even this simple story of her lost husband made Penelope weep. Just as the snows melted by the east wind run down the mountainside, so did the tears run down her lovely cheeks. Odysseus longed to comfort his wife, but he forced himself to remain silent.

When Penelope had spent her tears, she looked at Odysseus again. "Stranger, how shall I know if you speak the truth? If you truly have seen my husband, tell me—what did he look like? How was he clothed?"

"It has been twenty years, so my

memory of Odysseus is weak," said Odysseus. "But I will tell you how I remember him. He wore a thick purple cloak with a golden brooch. On the brooch were engraved a hound and a fawn."

Odysseus' words made Penelope weep even harder than before. "It was I who pinned that golden brooch to his purple cloak before he sailed away to war," she said through her sobs.

Odysseus could bear Penelope's tears no longer. "Please do not weep, my lady," he said. "I have heard recently that

Odysseus is alive, though all his men are dead. He will soon return home bearing great gifts. I believe he will come this very month, between the old moon and the new."

"I pray your words are true," said Penelope. "If they come to pass, you will be greatly honored."

The queen then called for her servants and told them to prepare a comfortable bed for the stranger.

"I have no need of a soft bed," Odysseus said. "I have long slept on the hard ground."

"Then at least allow my servant Euryclea to bathe you," said Penelope. "She cared for Odysseus from the day he was born until the day he sailed away to war."

Odysseus smiled and agreed to a bath. He sat silently by the firelight as Penelope took her leave and the old maidservant filled the water basin. As Euryclea began to bathe him, Odysseus remembered the scar above his knee. The scar was from a wound made by a boar's tusk when Odysseus was a young man. Before he could hide his leg, Euryclea saw the long white mark.

The old woman slowly traced her fingers over the scar. Then she looked up at Odysseus. Her eyes filled with tears. "Oh!" she whispered. "You are Odysseus!"

Odysseus grabbed Euryclea and pulled her close to him. "Woman, you must promise to tell no one who I am," he whispered fiercely, "until the gods have delivered these evil suitors into my hands."

"I promise," Euryclea whispered. "I shall be as silent as a stone."

After his bath, Penelope came to Odysseus again. "I fear the dark day has arrived," she said, "and I must finally marry one of these wretched men, or my son shall surely come to harm. So this is what I have decided to do. Long ago, my husband Odysseus could shoot a single arrow through the rings at the ends of twelve ax handles. Whoever among the suitors can string Odysseus' great bow and shoot with the same skill— he will I wed."

Odysseus nodded slowly. "I believe this is a good plan," he said. "Let the contest be held tomorrow."

Penelope smiled. "It is a great comfort to talk with you, my friend, but I must go to bed now. No mortal can go forever without sleep."

Odysseus watched Penelope climb the stairs to her chamber. Then he spread an oxhide on the floor of the hall and lay down to sleep.

But sleep would not come. Odysseus tossed restlessly, worrying about the coming fight. *I have suffered worse than this,* he thought. *I saw my own men hideously murdered by the Cyclops monster, and still*

I endured. I journeyed to the Land of the Dead. I survived storms and shipwrecks and escaped cannibal giants. . . . But no matter how he tried to reassure himself, Odysseus could not rest.

"Odysseus."

Odysseus opened his eyes. The goddess Athena was standing over him.

"Why can you not sleep?" she said. "Your wife is here, and so is your son. You are finally home."

"What you say is true," said Odysseus. "Yet I wonder if I can rid my home of these shameless suitors. They are always together in a great crowd. Even if I kill them all, surely others will come and try to avenge their deaths."

"Faithless mortal!" said the gray-eyed goddess. "Have I ever ceased to watch over you? Can we not defeat an *army* of men together? Go to sleep now. I promise you that with my help, you will prevail over your enemies."

FIVE

SIGNS FROM THE GODS

*O*dysseus awoke with the first light of day. When he heard the sounds of weeping coming from Penelope's chamber, a fresh wave of worry washed over him.

He lifted his hands and prayed to the

most powerful of the gods. "O Father Zeus," he whispered, "if it is your will that I win this battle today, please send me a sign."

A moment later, thunder rumbled in the clear blue heavens overhead.

A servant was grinding corn nearby. "Thunder!" she exclaimed. "And not a cloud in sight! Lord Zeus must be sending us a sign. May this be the last day that I slave for these terrible men!"

Odysseus was glad to hear her words and glad to hear the omen from the mighty god of the skies.

As dawn spread her rosy-fingered light throughout the rest of the palace, Telemachus rose from his bed and dressed for the coming battle. He slung his sword over his shoulder and tied on his sandals. He picked up his bronze-pointed spear and left his room.

In the courtyard outside, the suitors had again gathered to discuss how they might slay the young prince. But as they plotted against the son of Odysseus, a strange sight appeared in the sky: an eagle soared overhead, gripping a dove in its talons.

"Look!" said one of the suitors. "That is surely a bad omen for us! I fear it means our plot will fail!"

The other suitors shrugged off the sign and streamed into the great hall for their morning feast. As they passed around bowls of wine, Telemachus entered the hall with Odysseus. Still disguised as a beggar, Odysseus sat on a stool near the table. Telemachus poured wine into a bowl and offered it to the ragged man.

One of the suitors laughed and stood up. "Let *me* make a contribution to the beggar's bowl!" he said. Then he hurled a cow's foot through the air at Odysseus.

Odysseus ducked, then smiled through clenched teeth at his attacker. But Telemachus whirled on the rude suitor in fury. "You may eat from our table and drink from our wine barrels!" he shouted. "But you may not abuse a stranger in this noble house!"

The suitors all burst into laughter. Then a strange wind swept through the hall, carrying a spell from the goddess Athena. The suitors could not stop their laughter. As they howled uncontrollably, their blood seemed to spatter their food.

When they were finally able to regain control of themselves, one of the men leapt to his feet. "O lost men! I have just had a terrible vision, sent by the gods! I have seen what is to happen here today! I saw the walls of this room covered with blood! And I saw the table and halls filled with ghosts—ghosts hurrying to the darkness of the Land of the Dead. . . ."

SIX

STRINGING THE BOW

After breakfast, Penelope went to the storeroom of the palace and picked up the huge bow that had once belonged to Odysseus. She carried it out to the hall and set it down before all the suitors.

"Listen to me," she said to them. "For a long time, you have overrun this house. You have drunk my husband's wine and slaughtered his livestock. You say you are only waiting for me to choose one of you to marry. Well, here is your challenge. If one of you can string the bow of Odysseus and shoot an arrow through the rings of twelve ax handles in a row, that is the man I will marry."

The suitors eagerly took up the challenge. One by one, they tried to string Odysseus' mighty bow. But even though they greased it with hot tallow and warmed it near the fire, the strong bow would not bend.

While each suitor took his turn with the bow, the old swineherd and the cowherd who had long tended Odysseus' cattle slipped out of the hall. They were sickened by the sight of their enemies handling their master's bow.

Odysseus saw the two men go and hurried after them. "Wait!" he called. "I have a question for you both. If Odysseus were to drop from the sky and appear before you today, would you fight for him? Or would you fight on the side of the suitors?"

"Oh, if only Lord Zeus would hear my prayer and lead our master home," said the cowherd, "you would quickly see my strength in fighting for him."

The swineherd nodded and uttered his own desperate prayer for Odysseus' return.

Odysseus was certain he could trust his two old servants. "You must know, then, that your prayers have been answered," he said. "I am Odysseus. And if we defeat these suitors, I will honor you both."

The two men were speechless. They could not believe that the wretched beggar standing before them was truly their master, Odysseus.

Odysseus lifted his ragged cloak, revealing the long white scar above his knee. "Remember the wound inflicted by the tusk of the boar when I was young?" he asked.

The swineherd and cowherd fell upon their long-lost master and wept.

Odysseus embraced them. "Cease your tears now, or someone will see us and tell the others," he said. "Listen carefully to my orders. When we go back inside, give me the bow, so that I may have a turn in the contest. After I have it in my hands, make certain that all the women are locked in their rooms, and throw the bar across the courtyard gate."

When Odysseus and his two loyal servants returned to the great hall, they found that none of the suitors had been able to string the bow. "Why do you not resume your contest tomorrow?" Odysseus said. "Perhaps the archer god will help one of you then. But for now, let me hold that smooth bow. I should like to see if there is any force left in my hands, or if my hard travels have taken all my strength away."

The men reacted angrily. "You fool, do not dare to touch that bow," said Antinous. "Hold your tongue, or we will throw you out to sea."

Penelope stood up. "Our guest says he comes from a noble family," she said. "Give him the bow and let him try to string it."

"Mother, return to your chamber and your weaving," said Telemachus, for he knew that a bloody battle was about to begin. "I am master of this house. I will be the one to invite our guest to string the bow."

Penelope was surprised by the sharp words of her son, but she lowered her head and returned to her chamber. As she lay on her bed and wept for Odysseus, the goddess Athena closed Penelope's eyelids and sent her into a deep slumber, sparing her from the horror of what was about to happen.

In the great hall below, the swineherd and cowherd took the mighty bow and quiver of arrows and handed them to

Odysseus. Then they hurried from the room to give orders to the maids and lock the outside gate.

Odysseus slowly examined the bow. Then he bent and strung it effortlessly, as if he were a musician stringing a harp. When he finished, he plucked the taut cord. It sang like a swallow's note.

Thunder rumbled in the sky. Odysseus smiled, for he knew the thunder was another sign from the god Zeus. As the suitors watched in stunned silence, he picked up an arrow and set it against the bow. He aimed at the row of axes,

He drew the arrow back, and let it fly.

The arrow sailed perfectly through each of the twelve ax rings.

Odysseus put down his bow and looked at Telemachus. "The stranger you welcomed into your home has not disgraced you," he said.

Telemachus nodded. The battle was about to begin.

SEVEN

DEATH TO THE SUITORS

*O*dysseus threw off his rags and leapt onto the stone threshold of the hall. He glared down at the suitors.

"*That* contest is over," he said. "But now there is another target for my bow.

Help me, Apollo, god of archers—"
And with those words, Odysseus took
aim at Antinous, the leader of the
suitors, and sent an arrow straight into
the villain's throat.

As Antinous fell to the floor, the
other suitors sprang from their seats.
"You will pay for this!" one shouted at
Odysseus. "The vultures will soon eat
you!" They all then rushed about in great
confusion, searching for their weapons.
But no spears or shields could be found.

"Dogs!" Odysseus shouted at them.
"I—Odysseus—have come back! You

never thought you would see me again, did you? But now your final hour has come!"

"Use the tables for shields to block his arrows!" one of the suitors shouted. "Attack him with your swords!" The man rushed at Odysseus with his sword, but Odysseus swiftly slew him with another arrow from his bow.

Another suitor ran toward Odysseus, but Telemachus hurled his spear and killed him, too. Then Telemachus hurried from the room to get arms for the swine-herd and the cowherd.

Odysseus held off the suitors with his arrows until Telemachus returned with shields and spears and gave the weapons to their two allies. Then the four men stood together against the crowd.

One of Odysseus' enemies ran upstairs to the storeroom and found the door unlocked. He grabbed twelve spears and brought them to the others.

With the enemy now armed, it seemed impossible to Odysseus that he and his three comrades could defeat the scores of men. But suddenly the goddess Athena appeared in the hall.

"Join us in our fight!" Odysseus shouted to her.

Athena's eyes flashed. "You must prove yourselves first!" she said. Then she turned into a swallow and flew up to a roof beam to watch.

One after another, Odysseus sent his arrows streaking through the air, killing many of the suitors. Then he and his three comrades hurled their four spears at the enemy. When four of the suitors went down, Odysseus and his men pulled the spears from their bodies and hurled them again.

The suitors hurled spears, too. But Athena kept sending them astray. Finally the goddess sent a vision that struck terror into the suitors' hearts. A dark cloud appeared over the great hall. The cloud took the shape of Athena's mighty shield. The suitors knew that a vision of Athena's shield meant certain death.

Ruthlessly, Odysseus, Telemachus, and their two comrades slew man after man. Odysseus spared the life of the minstrel, for the singer sang songs sent from the gods. And he spared the herald, for he wanted him to spread the news that the men of this earth should do good and not evil.

But to all others, Odysseus showed no mercy. By the end of the battle, every suitor had been slain. Their bodies were heaped on the floor like dead fish thrown from a net onto the sand.

The god Hermes appeared in the great hall. Holding his golden wand, he led the suitors' ghosts from the palace.

Squeaking like bats, the ghosts followed Hermes over ocean waves.

They followed him past snowy rocks. They followed him beyond the sun's gate and beyond the place of dreams, until they arrived at last in the mist-shrouded Land of the Dead.

REUNION

Standing in a pool of blood, surrounded by the corpses of the suitors,
Odysseus called for the maidservant
Euryclea. When the old woman saw
the carnage, she shrieked with joy and

relief, for she knew the palace was finally free of the villains who had tormented Odysseus' family for so many years.

"Be silent," Odysseus commanded her. "It is wrong to exult over the dead."

"Let me at least go and tell Penelope," said the maid. "She has slept through the whole battle."

"No, do not wake her yet," said Odysseus. "Gather all the maids who once danced with the suitors. Order them to carry away the dead and wash the blood from the walls and floors."

Euryclea did as Odysseus commanded her. When the palace was scrubbed clean, Odysseus told her to make a fire to purify the house. Finally, as the fire sent its smoke through the halls and courtyard, Euryclea hurried upstairs to Penelope.

"Wake up!" she cried, shaking the sleeping queen. "Your beloved husband has returned! He waits for you now! Wake up!"

When Penelope opened her eyes, the old woman told her the story of the great battle and how she had found

Odysseus and Telemachus standing over the corpses of the suitors.

"Do not raise my hopes that it is truly Odysseus," said Penelope. "Surely, it is one of the immortal gods in disguise. My beloved husband is either far away on a distant island, or he is dead."

"Go and see for yourself!" urged Euryclea. "I saw the scar on his leg— from the tusk of the boar. Come with me now! He waits for you by his own fireside!"

"Old woman, you do not know the minds of the gods . . . or how they can trick us," said Penelope. "But I will go and see my son."

Penelope went downstairs. She found Odysseus sitting by the fire. His rags were covered with blood. Sweat and blood covered his dirty face and hair.

Stunned by Odysseus' savage appearance, Penelope turned away.

Telemachus rebuked her. "Mother, can you not even look at him? Is your heart so hard?"

But Odysseus was patient. He smiled and turned to Telemachus. "Let us wash ourselves and dress in fresh tunics," he said. "Then tell the minstrel to play a cheerful dance tune as if he were playing a wedding song. We must fool the neighbors, and delay the news of the slaughter from reaching the relatives of the slain. When they hear about it, they will surely seek revenge."

Odysseus left the hall, and servants bathed him and rubbed him with oil and dressed him in a clean tunic. Then the goddess Athena magically took away his beggar disguise and made him look younger and taller.

As handsome as a god, Odysseus

returned to the hearthside. He sat opposite Penelope. But still she was silent. Odysseus' transformation had made her even more mistrustful. Was this man truly a man? Or was he a god trying to deceive her?

"What a strange woman you are," said Odysseus. "After twenty years, you will not let your husband take you in his arms." When Penelope did not speak, Odysseus went on. "Well, then, I suppose I must sleep alone."

"What a strange man you are," said Penelope, "if indeed you are a man,

and not a god playing a trick on me."
Then Penelope thought of a trick of
her own. Long ago, Odysseus had built
their marriage bed from an olive
tree that grew through the floor of
their bedchamber. Only she and
Odysseus himself knew the secret
of its construction.

"I know not who you truly are,"
Penelope said, "but I will tell my maid to
prepare my own bed for you. Euryclea!"
she called, "have the servants place my
bed outside my chamber and pile it with
fleeces and sheets of linen."

Odysseus' eyes flashed with anger. "What happened to the bed I made for us long ago?" he said. "That bed could never be moved—one of its posts is the trunk of an olive tree still rooted in the ground! Has a thief cut that post and stolen our bed?"

Penelope gave a shout of joy and rushed into Odysseus' arms. "Only you would know this secret of our marriage bed!" she exclaimed tearfully. "Forgive me for doubting you!"

As his wife's arms closed tenderly about him, a deep ache rose in Odysseus' breast—the ache of a swimmer in a stormy sea who has long yearned for the sun-warmed earth. Holding Penelope in the flickering firelight of his own hearth, he wept with sweet grief.

As his mother and father embraced, Telemachus hushed the dancers and the servants. The hall was darkened, and everyone went to bed.

Odysseus and Penelope retired to their chamber, and to the bed with the post made from the olive tree. There they spent many hours of the night telling each other stories of all that had happened during Odysseus' absence.

While they talked, the goddess Athena held back the horses of Dawn—Firebright and Daybright—so the joyful couple could spend more time alone.

NINE

PEACE

*W*hen dawn finally came, Odysseus told Penelope that he must go to the country and see his father Laertes. Mad with grief, Laertes had mourned his lost son for twenty years. The old man refused even to live in the palace, preferring to sleep in rags in one of Odysseus' vineyards.

"While I am gone, lock yourselves and your maids in your rooms and speak to no one," Odysseus said to Penelope. "For I must warn you—by the end of this day, word will have spread about the death of the suitors—and their kin will surely come seeking revenge."

Odysseus then woke Telemachus, and the swineherd and cowherd, and asked them to go with him to see his father. Though it was bright morning when they set out, Athena shrouded the four men in darkness until they came to Laertes' vineyard far from town.

"Go to the house and prepare a meal for us," Odysseus told the others. "I will go into the fields and find my father."

In one of the fields of the vineyard, Odysseus saw an old man hoeing the ground. Bent over his hoe, the man wore a filthy tunic and a tattered hat made of goatskin. It grieved Odysseus to see his father Laertes looking so weary and ragged.

"Forgive me for disturbing you," Odysseus called out. "I am looking for a friend of mine. He once stopped at my island and stayed in our house. He said he was from Ithaca and that his father was Laertes."

The old man lowered his head and wept. "That must have been my son, my unfortunate son, Odysseus," he said. "He has long been dead. Far from home, he was eaten by the fish of the sea or perhaps by wild beasts on land."

"Indeed?" said Odysseus. "It has only been a few years since I saw him. I gave him gifts and sent him on his way. I thought the omens for him were good.

We had every hope of meeting again."

Laertes nodded and his eyes filled with tears. Then the burden of his grief became too much for him. Groaning with misery, he picked up a handful of dirt and poured it over his head.

Odysseus could not bear to see his father suffer a moment longer. He rushed forward and threw his arms around the sad old man. "Father, I am your son," he said. "I have returned. And I have destroyed all those who tormented you and my wife and son."

Laertes stammered in disbelief. "Can—

can you give me proof that you are truly my son?" he asked.

"I can show you this hunting wound," said Odysseus, revealing the scar above his knee. "And I can tell you about the trees in your orchards. When I was a boy, you gave me thirteen pear trees and ten apple trees and forty fig trees."

Hearing these words, Laertes collapsed to the ground in a faint. Odysseus held his father tightly to his chest, until Laertes opened his eyes again. A smile of joy spread over the old man's face—then a look of fear.

"I am afraid that soon the families of the slain suitors will come seeking revenge," said Laertes.

"Do not worry about them now," said Odysseus. "Come, let us go to the farmhouse and have a meal together with your grandson, Telemachus."

Odysseus helped his father to the house, where a great feast awaited them. There the old man bathed and dressed in a fine cloak. The goddess Athena gave youthful energy to his frail limbs and made him taller and stronger.

In the midst of their celebration, an angry shout came from outside. Armed men had indeed come seeking revenge for the death of the suitors.

Odysseus, his father, and his son quickly pulled on armor and went outside. Laertes hurled his spear through the air and killed one of the men. Odysseus and Telemachus held up their swords and prepared to meet their enemy.

At that moment, Athena appeared. "Hold back!" she cried. "Stop, before another drop of blood is shed!"

Odysseus' foes turned pale at the sight of the great goddess. They dropped their weapons and fled in terror. Odysseus let out a savage battle cry. He swooped like an eagle after them.

But mighty Zeus threw a thunderbolt to earth. Seeing this sign, Athena called Odysseus back. "Cease fighting, Odysseus, before you anger the gods!" she cried. "All fighting must end! Let there be peace from now on!"

Odysseus was relieved to hear these words. He gladly gave up the pursuit of his enemies. He knew that with the blessing of the gods, all his battles were over—battles against Trojan warriors, against monsters of the deep, against terrible storms, and against enemies at home. Odysseus had survived each and every one, and was finally reunited with his beloved family.

From that day on, and for many years to come, peace reigned on the island of Ithaca, and the gods looked favorably upon Odysseus, his wife, and his son.

ABOUT HOMER AND THE ODYSSEY

Long ago, the ancient Greeks believed that the world was ruled by a number of powerful gods and goddesses. Stories about the gods and goddesses are called the Greek myths. The myths were probably first told as a way to explain things in nature—such as weather, volcanoes, and constellations. They were also recited as entertainment.

The first written record of the Greek myths comes from a blind poet named Homer. Homer lived almost three thousand years ago. Many believe that Homer was the author of the world's two most famous epic poems: the *Iliad* and the *Odyssey*. The *Iliad* is the story of the Trojan War. The *Odyssey* tells about the long journey of Odysseus, king of an island called Ithaca. The tale concerns Odysseus' adventures on his way home from the Trojan War.

To tell his tales, Homer seems to have drawn upon a combination of his own imagination and Greek myths that had been passed down by word of mouth. A bit of actual history may have also gone into Homer's stories; there is archaeological evidence to suggest that the story of the Trojan War was based on a war fought about five hundred years before Homer's time.

Over the centuries, Homer's *Odyssey* has greatly influenced the literature of the Western world.

GODS AND GODDESSES OF ANCIENT GREECE

The most powerful of all the Greek gods and goddesses was Zeus, the thunder god. Zeus ruled the heavens and the mortal world from a misty mountaintop known as Mount Olympus. The main Greek gods and goddesses were all relatives of Zeus. His brother Poseidon was ruler of the seas, and his brother Hades was ruler of the underworld. His wife Hera was queen of the gods and goddesses. Among his many children were the gods Apollo, Mars, and Hermes, and the goddesses Aphrodite, Athena, and Artemis.

The gods and goddesses of Mount Olympus not only inhabited their mountaintop but also visited the earth, involving themselves in the daily activities of mortals such as Odysseus.

THE MAIN GODS
AND GODDESSES
AND PRONUNCIATION
OF THEIR NAMES

Zeus (zyoos), king of the gods, god of thunder

Poseidon (poh-SY-don), brother of Zeus, god of seas and rivers

Hades (HAY-deez), brother of Zeus, king of the Land of the Dead

Hera (HEE-ra), wife of Zeus, queen of the Olympian gods and goddesses

Hestia (HES-tee-ah), sister of Zeus, goddess of the hearth

Athena (ah-THEE-nah), daughter of Zeus, goddess of wisdom and war, arts and crafts

Demeter (dih-MEE-tur), goddess of crops and the harvest, mother of Persephone

Aphrodite (ah-froh-DY-tee), daughter of Zeus, goddess of love and beauty

Artemis (AR-tem-is), daughter of Zeus, goddess of the hunt

Ares (AIR-eez), son of Zeus, god of war

Apollo (ah-POL-oh), god of the sun, music, and poetry

Hermes (HUR-meez), son of Zeus, messenger god, a trickster

Hephaestus (heh-FEES-tus), son of Hera, god of the forge

Persephone (pur-SEF-uh-nee), daughter of Zeus, wife of Hades and queen of the Land of the Dead

Dionysus (dy-oh-NY-sus), god of wine and madness

PRONUNCIATION GUIDE TO OTHER PROPER NAMES

Argus (AR-guss)

Antinous (an-TIN-oh-us)

Calypso (cah-LIP-soh)

Crete (KREET)

Euryclea (yoo-rih-CLAY-ah)

Ithaca (ITH-ah-kah)

Laertes (LAY-er-teez)

Menelaus (men-eh-LAY-us)

Minos (MEE-nohss)

Odysseus (oh-DIS-yoos)

Penelope (pen-EL-oh-pee)

Telemachus (Tel-EM-ah-kus)

Trojans (TROH-junz)

A NOTE ON THE SOURCES

The story of the Odyssey was originally written down in the ancient Greek language. Since that time there have been countless translations of Homer's story into other languages. I consulted a number of English translations, including those written by Alexander Pope, Samuel Butler, Andrew Lang, W.H.D. Rouse, Edith Hamilton, Robert Fitzgerald, Allen

Mandelbaum, Robert Fagles, and E. V. Rieu.

Homer's *Odyssey* is divided into twenty-four books. The sixth volume of *Tales from the Odyssey* was derived from books 16-24 (with brief references to the events that take place in books 9-12).

ABOUT THE AUTHOR

MARY POPE OSBORNE is the author of the best-selling Magic Tree House series. She has also written many acclaimed historical novels and retellings of myths and folktales, including *Favorite Greek Myths* and *American Tall Tales.* She lives with her husband, Will, in northeastern Connecticut.

Zeus

Hera

Artemis

Hephaestus

Apollo

Ares

Athen

GODS and GODDESSES of ANCIENT GREECE

Hermes

Dionysus

Aphrodite

Hestia

Demeter

Persephone

Poseidon

Hades